The Tale of Dribbles

Cody Toye

Copyright©2014

Blood Moon Press

ISBN-13 978-0615989068

ISBN-10: 0615989063

Blood Moon Press

"Don't stick it to the man. Become the man and laugh with morbid understanding as he becomes...you."

Dedication

To Donna Jacques.

I shall not forget 3:30 am, the cold,
Nor the infinite amount of yogurt.

It was truly the worst and the best.

*****

Operation Coffee Deprivation

"After watching your performance this quarter and keeping a close eye on our profit margin, we have decided to let you go. You have served our blah to the fullest blah and blah blah." Bob watched the bald spot pulse as Mr. Jefferson attempted to explain why he was firing him after twenty five years. In the business world, Bob was a little slow. He focused primarily on computer programming and didn't care about profit margins.

A small chuckle hiccupped out of his throat as he remembered the picture he had encrypted into the last email of his career. The bald head of Mr. Jefferson appeared with a nice black line through it. The line, perfectly drawn over the rough bald noggin portrayed his true feelings for the man. Every time the email gets forwarded, the recipient would be in for a surprise. Bob was certain the butt crack joke would be seen by all the big spenders before it was said and done. This thought alone was better than anything they could offer him for his time.

Anger crept into his blood stream, turning his complexion a strawberry tint. The more words that spewed from the mouth of the traitor, the harder it became to concentrate. The blah blahs were replaced with a fictitious underlying meaning.

"So... in short Bob, I am a jerk! I'm ugly and bald and make three times your salary. I will get a huge bonus if I fire you. I will then pay someone six dollars and hour less to do your job. I know it was you pooping in the plant holders in the lobby, (it was) so security will show you out. Oh, by the way Bob, My brand new red Porsche is not scratch proof, so feel free to use your sharpest car keys to teach me a lesson!"

A large sigh squeezed its way out of his lungs. This, followed by the slow movement of his defeated body rising from the cold wooden chair was the only response he could manage. He knew Mr. Jefferson didn't say anything remotely close to that but didn't care. One black loafer in front of the other he walked. He walked slowly to the door feeling the dead glare of an over-rated man burrow into the back of his skull.

Two sharply dressed security officers waited for him on the other side of the door. Slowly, the curvy golden handle of the office door turned. Slam. Slam. After the third hard smash, Bob managed to get escorted down the long corridor towards the lobby. The checkered marble seemed to taunt him as shame grew deep within. The colors seemed even more vivid than he remembered.

Stomping past the water fountain, he spotted three corporate slackers telling the same jokes as always. He slowly turned towards them with a crooked smile upon his face. By now, he was sure that word had swept through the office at sub-atomic speeds. Not only that, but it managed to make it to Jupiter and back. Right now some poor schmuck of an alien is pointing his finger down to Earth and laughing at him. They all knew, he was sure of it.

Silence fell upon the room. They were waiting on him to leave. Waiting on him to hold his head down in shame and march out of the office. He was going to have none of it... no way... not a chance.

[4]

Bob did the opposite. Standing upon the shadows of three very important men, something very unexpected happened. He laughed. He not only laughed but gasped for air. Tears streamed down his cheeks and his foot thumped against the floor echoing through the entire room.

About the time he started dipping his tie into the water fountain and sucking the water off, those same nicely dressed security guards walked him out of his office for good. The Last thing anyone remembers Bob saying that day was "Beware of the squirrels in diapers, they don't understand Greek." Bob slowly walked towards the yellow curb. Random thoughts plagued him as he sat down and wept. "Twenty five years of my life gone." He thought glumly of the memories from his years of servitude and found it ironic how much time was spent wishing for a different job.

*****

Life went on at Q.J. Enterprises and after awhile everyone forgot about poor Bob. They went about their day like any good zombie would. As for Bob, he remembered every single one of them. He became consumed with hatred so deep that he spent every penny he had on revenge. He wasn't crazy that day, oh no, he knew exactly what he was saying. He wasn't crazy at all, just very well organized. His whole retirement fund was spent at a local pet store. Two hundred squirrels had found a new home that day; all of them recruited into Bob's army.

It took two months to do it, but Bob finished his computer program. He used images of acorns, walnuts, and others to brain-wash his miniature minions. Squirrel after squirrel ran his elaborate obstacle course, learning how to do specific tasks. Then there was the best of the best, the Green Beret of the squirrel world. This squad, led by Dribbles the squirrel, learned a multitude of tasks that needed to be carried out. One by one he worked with them all until they were ready to take on the world. He started small, experimenting on local citizens. His mission was simple: minor annoyance.

The sun was shining brightly that morning when Bob loaded his mini-van of doom. A warm fuzzy feeling exploded deep within his stomach. For the first time in a very long time, Bob was in a great mood! The mini-van swept across the bi-pass at tremendous speeds. He turned the music up full blast, forcing the sound to penetrate his glass windows and keep the outside world company. His head slowly bobbed to the music while weaving in and out of traffic. Mrs. Smith did not know how to react to what just happened.

She was in the middle of her morning commute, doing her usual talk on the cell phone and drive routine. All of a sudden, a mini-van with speeds exceeding seventy miles per hour weaved in front of her. This would have been normal, except the middle aged man behind the wheel was head banging to Mozart. She watched as the maniac did the same thing to the next two cars in line. His excess speeds then slowed to a crawl as he very carefully made a left into the Public Library. All she could do was shake her head. "It must have been something he ate," she thought. The small red mini-van pulled into an isolated spot and parked.

*****

Students came in and out, never once bothering to give him the time of day. The cool wind and warm spring sun drew a large crowd into the outside world. "A perfect day for a test run," he thought to himself. Bob opened the door to his van and stretched his legs. He felt the excitement build as he opened the back door and released the lock on the cage. The clink of freedom sent Dribbles flying out of his cage in a panic. He jumped, he scurried, he flicked his cute bushy tail then disappeared behind a large shrub.

Jimmy had just finished his homework and was shuffling his books back and forth, jockeying for a good grip. A balancing act that was almost impossible to perform. Papers tried their best to fly away, but to no avail. Four hours in a library simply meant that Jimmy was more determined to keep the papers than the wind was to take them from him. "One more Saturday gone forever!" he thought to himself. A sigh of relief and a sense of accomplishment overwhelmed his senses. He thought he might never get to see another weekend as a free man, but this is the last assignment he has to turn in. "This is it," he thought as he slowly made it down the sidewalk towards his freedom "I am done"

At first Jimmy had no idea what had happened. A furry brown blur streaked across his line of sight momentarily confusing him. Books flew to the ground, papers scattered in the wind, and Jimmy stood there shocked, mouth open and eyes bugged. "Wow, that squirrel is a Jerk" he thought to himself. A quick flick and a brief jump, Dribbles lay his head down inside the cage.

*****

"It worked, my program actually worked!" the sinister smile felt comfortable on his face as visions of what lay ahead appeared in a thick fog before him. Clink.

[9]

Clink. Bob locked the cage and headed home. The drive seemed to never end and impatience swelled deep inside. "One hour to prepare, one hour to exact my revenge!" The sweat retreated from his forehead as he led every single squirrel into their steal prison cells. Two hundred cages turned his living room into a perpetual petting zoo. The lack of space in his vehicle meant he would have to take one mission at a time. Bob rattled happy thoughts around his cranium, realizing it would be better this way. "I can make them suffer, over and over again!" He understood how sadistic it was to torture them over a long period of time but didn't care.

"No less than they deserve. Did they care that I missed out on a raise three years in a row? Did they care when they fired me without even blinking?" Bob recalled every little detail of their treachery and was replaying it over and over in his mind. Cartoons flowed through his mind like water through a faucet. A strange, yet satisfying version of Spy vs. Spy twisted his thoughts. In this version though, the black spy was a squirrel, and the white spy stays huddled in the corner crying for his mommy.

*****

The morning sun just peaked over the horizon when Art pulled into his usual parking spot. A sanctuary he began to call his home over the years. One more "hair check" and he was off to start the day. The smell of the dew on the grass and the glimmer of the golden sign above the revolving door reminded him of how great it was to be him. As he pushed into the lobby a whole heard of "Good morning Mr. Conway" resonated in his ear canals. With a smile upon his face he headed towards his private office.

He no more than relaxed his body in his Italian Leather chair when the door creaked open. The sound of the un-oiled hinges grated on his nerves. "This early in the morning no one should have to hear that!" He thought to himself.

"Here's your cup of coffee Mr. Conway."

Art slowly took the coffee from his secretary and placed it upon his desk. The steam started fogging up his glasses in an instant. "Thank you Janelle." He said through a smile.

"You're very welcome Sir. If there is anything else I can help with don't hesitate to ask." Janelle forced a smile back but was having trouble coping with her personal assistant position. "Four years of college and I become a secretary? How fair is that?" She muttered under her breath. Her foot no more than graced the presence of the doorway when his voice called to her.

"There is something you can help me with. I have several meetings and a deadline to meet today; if you can oil my door I would appreciate it."

"No problem Sir" she muttered. What, now I am the maintenance man too? If I could just tell him off…but bills have to get paid. She started to angrily stomp out the door when she was interrupted once again.

"Oh, and Janelle…"

She turned to face him, trying to keep very calm. Inhale and exhale wwwooosh. "Yes Sir"

"If you could keep the coffee coming it would make my day. Long hours ahead of me you know" Art smiled once again, but this time she could tell it was a simple power play, a gesture to show that he is in control and she is nothing more than a servant.

"No problem sir!" Came the short reply. With that, she snuck quietly out into the lobby.

Art drank his coffee and worked on his memos all day long. The sun beat high in the sky, casting a light shadow through his window. The clock ticked with all its might and tocked as well. Finally, noon rolled around. To Art, this meant lunchtime was upon him. He knew this not because the clock struck high noon, but because he said so. He didn't need the clock to tell him it was lunch-time, he was in control, he told the clock it was lunch-time. His stomach just dictated when he would do so. Today, his stomach says lunchtime is at noon. He marched through the office enjoying his normal chit-chat with the worker bees and had his fifteen minutes of cooler talk before heading to the lobby.

The lobby, in its own fanciful way, was a replica of how he felt inside himself today. The warm glow of the gold inlays and the marble counter tops showed elegance and power. After all, who's more elegant and powerful than a Chief Executive Officer of Q.J. Enterprises? He thought to himself.

Looking around the room, he noticed how happy everyone seemed to be at that moment. What Art couldn't understand is the why. Why were they okay sharing lunchtime fables with other worker bees? Why are they happy with the horrible paychecks we give them? Finally, why don't they ever talk to me? This was the ultimate why and to Art, this was a hard one. "I make more money than them, I have my own office, I am an interesting man. Why do they never invite me to sit down and share lunchtime fables?" For a moment, sadness tried to hitch a ride on the emotion train.

This was very brief though, as it only took a moment longer for him to realize who he was.

An hour later and a stomach fuller, he made his way back to his office. Meetings came and went but his work seemed to pile up on him. His eyes, now fully packed for vacation, started to show bags. He drank his coffee all day but it didn't seem to help.

He slowly dragged his heavy finger to the intercom and pushed the large button. He knew this was the right button because he forced his secretary to test it three times this week. Just like last week, the button has not moved. "Janelle. Janelle, can you come in here please?" Thick static is the only reply he got. Wait…noise came from the magic box after all. On the other end was a deep voice with a Hispanic accent.

"Janelle went home sick today Mr. Conway." Krrrhh. "Is there anything I can do?"

"Never mind I'll do it myself." He released the button and rushed through the door. Bam. The sound of wood on wood startled everyone within a ten cubicle radius. Phone calls were put on hold, sentences left unuttered. Everyone stopped what they were doing to watch this spectacle. "They don't pay me enough" he grumbled "Imagine, me, Mr. Conway, making my own coffee. Someone should get fired that's what I say. Grumble, grumble, grumble.

Everyone knew if they snickered they were canned. Everyone in the vicinity bit their lower lips as the great Mr. Conway... smarter than they would ever hope to be... fought bravely with the coffeepot and lost. Water overflowed, filters fell from the cabinet making a huge mess all over the floor. After about ten minutes he managed to get it right and reached up into the cabinet to pull down the coffee. That was the moment of his undoing.

Four cabinets and a drawer opened simultaneously dropping supplies all over the place. Every container of coffee fell to the floor exploding into a mini bean mushroom cloud. Sugar fell from sky; coffee- filters and stir-sticks danced briefly in the air before settling down for the night. The whole area looked like the aftermath of a natural disaster on a destructive rampage.

Then, five pesky squirrels in diapers bounced off of the cabinet and disappeared into the quiet office. Art just stood there. The initial shock left him confused and angry. He marched through the ten cubicles and into his office. He sat quietly for a brief moment, trying to calm the rising anger. The more he tried, the worse it got. The wildlife wants to play games, let's play! He thought. First, he pulled up the order sheet and ordered more office supplies; then he hired an exterminator. "I'll give you a reason to wear those diapers!" He mumbled faster and faster until his order was ready to get placed.

His fat finger came crashing down onto something cold. "Cold? Is that right?" When he glanced down he noticed his 'Enter' key was missing. To the logical mind, this is nothing more than an inconvenience. After all, you can still hit 'Enter' without the key can't you? That's not quite how it works though. Art is far too important to use logic. That is why he pays his workers! The world would have to end before he used an incomplete keyboard.

He threw his pencil holder across the room making an even bigger mess. Now, in the office next to him, he got ready to boot up the computer. No 'Enter' key. "You have got to be kidding me," he thought as he stomped back into the cubicle area. "Nope, nope, nope, and nope." Not a single keyboard had the almighty 'Enter'. In a panic, He rushed back to his office, about killing the fern that adorned the waiting room. His finger, now shaking, pressed the big button once more. "Mr. Jefferson. Mr. Jefferson? Mr. Jefferson, pick up. This is Art. This is an emergency! Mr. Jefferson, pick up." No answer.

*****

Dribbles clung tightly to the wildly swinging intercom wires like Tarzan's pet rodent. Mr. Jefferson was none the wiser. Only one floor below him, the entire accounting department was in chaos. Bob loved it. The scene unfolded through two tiny binocular lenses, his beloved Dribbles was poised for phase two.

The sun beat down on him; leaving sweat stains on his new shirt. Bob did not care. This was worth it. To him, watching his plan work perfectly may have its costs, but it was worth every bead of sweat his body could produce. The Mini-van stayed parked on the far edge the parking lot which was reserved for the lower class new hires. No one ever pays attention to the inhabitants here.

Bob opens his door letting the fresh air invade the confined space. What a wonderful day it turned out to be. The birds chirped a happy chirp, the sun smiled and the shrubs stood proud, showing off their new manicures. His legs screamed at him as they tried to support the weight of the rest of his body. Several hours in the cramped cab takes its toll.

He trudged, one step at a time, towards the back hatch. When he was certain no one was watching he lifted it with a mighty pull. The chattering of the twenty squirrels was music to his ears. They twitched their little noses and flicked their bushy tails. A sign they were ready to obey.

Bob felt the heat radiate off of the metal wires of the cages. Silence fell upon the mini-van. Forty blank beady eyes stared at their master, hoping and waiting for their freedom. "That's right, I am your Master. Obey me tiny minions and destroy all I oppose. Mwahaha." His words echoed back into his ears, scaring poor Bob.

His thumb and first finger wrapped around the latches releasing chaos, one by one, into Q.J. Enterprise. The second wave has begun. The squirrels scurried across the blacktop, zigzagging back and forth. Some jumped over the shrubs, others ran through it. Nothing would distract them from their goals.

What a sight to see, Bob couldn't stop smiling as he watched twenty overfed squirrels try to wedge themselves into the rain gutter. He hoped everything would go as planned, but as life taught him, it rarely did.

Panic set in as he watched fifteen squirrels make it inside the gutter. The sixteenth one was not so lucky. It pushed. It scratched. It got its fat furry butt wedged in the opening. The squirrel flailed its tail back and forth and produced a screeching sound that reminded him of a cross between fingernails on a blackboard and an off-balanced washing machine. This sound was sure to draw attention.

The stress built-up and squeezed Bob's heart muscle. His chest lifted and lowered. Bob watched anxiously, hoping the other four squirrels would be smart enough to gain access through an alternate route. No luck! The other four squirrels piled upon each other trying to climb into the rain gutter. Each attempt forced a louder shriek to ricochet through the gutter. After having exhausted all their energy, four fat furry squirrels gave up.

Bob watched as they curled up and went to sleep right where they stood and where they could easily be spotted. "You got to be kidding me!" Bob slumped down in his chair hoping to become invisible. Things couldn't get worse.

*****

Mr. Jefferson swiveled his chair to face the flat screen monitor. He nimbly adjusted his tie and straightened his marble and gold name plate. His meeting with Mr. Matsumoto is about to begin and he only has one chance for a great impression. This account is worth millions and he can't afford to blow it.

Once more, he checked his files. The email detailing his marketing budget and labor costs was sent at exactly 2:05 pm. Files, check. Name plate, check. Best suit and tie in my wardrobe, check. "What could

I be missing? Think. Think." He turned his chair around in a smooth arc and micro-adjusted the family portrait that stood on the shelf behind him. After making sure it would be visible during the video-conference, Mr. Jefferson assumed the position in front of the monitor.

Mr. Matsumoto is a family man. Family values are very important to us at Q.J. Enterprise. Important enough to fake for a short duration while the business man forks over enough money to carry by the shovel-full. "Here we go." Mr. Jefferson inhaled deeply one last time before turning the monitor on. With a fake smile on his face, he waited patiently for the conference to begin.

"Mr. Matsumoto, how wonderful it is to finally meet you!"

"The honor is all mine, Mr. Jefferson."

The Japanese business man sighs in disgust as he notices the family portrait adorning the shelf behind him. Americans always put on cheap, fleeting values to impress him. He knew from the reports that Mr. Jefferson was recently divorced. An act such as this says something to him, it says that Mr. Jefferson must think he is dumb enough to invest without researching any weakness in the company. Shame on him. Let's get this over with, he thought to himself.

"I have been looking over your quarterly reports, Mr. Jefferson, and I must say, pretty impressive work. I do however, wonder how much of my money will be spent on advertising and wages."

The moment was at hand, He could not help but to gloat internally. Mr. Jefferson took great strides to lower labor costs and abuse statistics in his favor. This email meant a big promotion; he could feel it in his bones.

"I have sent an email detailing how much of your hard earned money will be spent. Better than that, Mr. Matsumoto, I have outlined how much more money will come flooding into your bank account. Check your inbox."

The silence was unbearable as the screen turned blue. Mr. Matsumoto checked out momentarily while he searched his emails. Mr. Jefferson did a little happy dance and crossed his fingers. I have him by the wallet now, he smugly thought. Click. The screen turned back on. Excitement built inside Mr. Jefferson, knowing good things were ahead. The reply baffled him.

Laughing… large bursts of laughter. This is the reply he got from the Japanese investor. On the screen he saw one skinny finger point at the computer and snorting a laugh. Mr. Jefferson worked so hard to manipulate these statistics, this is not acceptable.

"Do you see the potential our company has Mr. Matsumoto? I can personally build the bridge to financial security for the both of us". No reply came from the investor. Instead, more laughter came rumbling over the screen. "I know we are new at this Mr. Matsumoto, but it is not our custom to laugh at potential partners. Would you like to share what is so funny?"

Taking large gasps of breath and wiping the corner of his eyes with a monogrammed silk handkerchief, the reply came flooding out, "You are a butt-head."

"I beg your pardon? Did I hear you right?"

The face of the American Finance Director became as bright as a rose in springtime. His face scrunched and his teeth clenched.

"You are a butt-head, Mr. Jefferson."

"If you don't want to invest, Mr. Matsumoto, then just say so. I will not tolerate being insulted."

"The email you sent me has nothing but a picture of your head made out to look like a butt. Call us back when you become a professional."

Click. The last thing he heard was giggles from the world's largest industrial investor. He could almost hear the money being flushed down a large toilet. How sad. He didn't think his day could get any worse. He spun around in his chair and flung the family portrait across the room shattering the glass and making a huge mess.

His precious finger came crashing down on the intercom button. He had never needed a drink as badly as he needed right now. "Lindsey, could you bring me a scotch? Lindsey?" No reply. "What is wrong with this blasted thing? Just great." He knelt down in his five hundred dollar suit to look for a solution.

He could go get his own drink, but decided to fix the intercom instead. His hand traced the back of the intercom feeling the cool edges. He felt an empty hole where the cord calls home. As he examined his office further, he found the cord sleeping on the job. If it was an employee, it would be on the unemployment train by now. With a gentle click, the two ends were forced to meet. "There, that should do it. At least something is going right." He mumbled. He smashed the button once more; sure his Scotch would be in his hands momentarily.

"Lindsey, could you bring me a ..." Complete darkness surrounded him. A black-out at high noon.

*****

Dribbles clung to the plastic switch controlling the second floor, a balancing act between the ground and the breaker box. Bob watched from the van, as the entire quadrant darkened. "Certainly this will still work. I mean, we are only short five squirrels. Stupid squirrels." He watched as the maintenance man came stomping out the front doors on a mission.

*****

He was to fix the electricity or else. So says Mr. Jefferson. He inhaled the fresh air, breathing deeply, trying to purge the lack of self-respect.

"Fifteen years with the company and they don't even know my name," he grumbled to himself. His hand instinctively slid over the patch embroidered onto his coveralls. Conway. That's funny. I spent the last thirty five years as Craig. Apparently my name changed to Conway when I sold my soul to this company.

Fix the electric Conway, Fix the plumbing Conway, punch me in the face and call me an ass-hole Craig! Um…Conway. My application was for the Accounting department. I hold a Bachelor's degree in Business Management and an Associate's degree in Accounting. Many qualifications for a top position here, but the biggest qualification of all is my handle-bar mustache. It states that I know how to fix things big and small without hesitation. I can barely change a light bulb, let along fix the electric.

A job is a job. A large depressing sigh came barreling out, forcing his muscles to loosen and his body to slump. His hand released the tool from his tool belt. His friends call this a Crescent Wrench; he calls it the chompy thingy mcbob that keeps banging into his hip.

He took one big step over the sleeping squirrels trying not to disturb them. He knew they were there, but didn't care. It wasn't his job to remove pests. Besides, he thought to himself, maybe they will attack Mr. Jefferson. That would be awesome. He could picture five squirrels completely destroying his office and breaking the pictures adorning the shelves behind him.

The gnawing and gnawing of wood and metal would be music to my ears. They would chew up all the superficial accomplishments the man had bestowed upon himself. He would swat, he would swear, and he would scream for Lindsey to save him. When he was at his breaking point, I would rush in there and say "Mr. Jefferson, I wish I could help you, but you told me this morning not to do anything that was not in my job description. You don't pay me to think. Just repair the electric. Yep, the electric is fine in here, have a good day!" I think I will leave them sleeping.

Bob watched in amazement as the maintenance man stepped over the squirrels as if it was an everyday occurrence. Things somehow managed to work themselves out. Bob smiled. Conway slowly walked around the corner of the office building, avoiding the shrubs that hug the sidewalk.

When he got to the breaker box, a tiny squirrel in a diaper scurried up the massive Oak tree. He didn't even pause. Why not? he thought to himself. He flipped the breaker and with a loud click, power was restored to the second floor.

*****

When the lights came back on, a loud cheer rose from the workers. This lasted exactly thirty seconds. Nothing but the computer and printer remained on their desks. The staplers, the paperclips, the white-out, and even the tiny pushpins that lay in waiting on the corkboards mounted on the cubicle walls behind them were gone.

The worker bees where in an uproar! Screams and threats came like a barrage of cannonballs towards the workers next to them. Something had to be done. Mr. Jefferson knew exactly what to do.

"Lindsey... Lindsey, could you come in here please? Lindsey?" His finger pressed the button harder and harder but no reply came.

He lifted the intercom off of his desk, watching the cord sway back and forth. The copper wires gleamed in the florescent light; tiny plastic bits were sheared off in small chunks. It had been gnawed through. For the second time today, Mr. Jefferson could feel his blood pressure shoot to dangerous levels.

His hands straightened the toupee that attempted to cover his bald head, making him feel just a little better about himself. With a grunt and a little effort, he rose from his Italian Leather rump rest. He no more than straightened his body when darkness suffocated his surroundings. He dexterously found his way to the double paned window. With a little effort, he heaved it open and yelled at the top of his lungs "CONWAY! FIX THE ELECTRIC!"

*****

He just exited the elevator on the second floor when he heard it. Little scratchy noises. Little scratchy noises followed by the devil bidding for his attention. Everything was dark once again. His handle-bar mustache twitched and stretched as he attempted a smile. I love those squirrels! He thought to himself. His footsteps were slow and steady, as he navigated the dark office. After about five minutes of touch and go, he made it to the sunlight.

His eyes struggled to accommodate the invasion of light in pupils, making his job just that much harder. He calmly walked back to the breaker-box and flipped the little switch. Immediately the lights came back on... Conway sat down on the curb and lit a cigarette. The smoke swirled deep into his lungs. He was in no hurry. Conway knew the lights would go out once again. Right on cue, the little squirrel came running down the Oak tree and straight towards him. This is awesome! He thought.

*****

Mr. Jefferson was relieved when the darkness was vanquished. The fear was paralyzing. As the only big-wig that is afraid of the dark, he thought, I must maintain my composure. He once again stood and attempted to straighten his hair piece. A damp and sticky residue ran down his bald head.

Something was different. A black blob slowly scurried across the gleaming floor. It made it under the door and out into the general population. BANG. The door flew open and a very angry Mr. Jefferson scurried behind it. Laughter erupted. Fingers were pointed. Every worker suddenly forgot why they were mad to begin with. It zigged, it zagged, it ran underneath cubicles. Mr. Jefferson was just a bit faster.

He huffed, he grunted, and he dove seconds before his toupee made it out into the lobby. He had it now. He hung onto it with all his might and felt it struggle beneath his grip. Loud chirpy squeaky sounds rang out, but he did not care. Nobodies hair, not even his own, will make a mockery of the great Mr. Jefferson.

Little clicks and flashes came as employees took pictures from their cell phones. Tomorrow, he would be a YouTube star! Darkness forced his grip loose. He could hear the daring hair escape from him.

*****

"CONWAY!" The little man watched the squirrel once again scurry up the mighty Oak. Click. He flipped the switch once more. As he sat down, he wondered if he had ever had an easier job.

*****

It happened so fast that it blew his mind. One moment he was struggling with his toupee, the next it was dangling from the ceiling fan ten feet in the air. In the span of only a few seconds, every keyboard had been stripped down to its bare essentials. The cords all have been chewed through on the phones and intercom system.

Not a single trace of any office supply remained. One thing became very clear, Q.J. Enterprise was under attack. With one big piqued step, Mr. Jefferson headed through the lobby and towards the elevator. Loud bursts of angry complaints threatened to tear down the very fabric of existence of the mighty empire.

He was sure if he didn't get to the bottom of this soon; he would have many workers leave, never to return. The stares of uncertainty burned into him as he passed by. Blame was a powerful weapon. A weapon when wielded correctly can turn the most successful man into a pile of mush in just mere moments. He felt the sting. He felt the blame cut deep. With each step, hushed whispers and indignant laughs brought him to his boiling point.

He just passed the fern near the waiting area and made it into the elevator when he first heard the chattering. As the metal doors started to squeeze shut, he caught a glimpse of many brown furry bodies scamper into view. Now isolated from the insanity, Mr. Jefferson started to relax. Isolation never felt so good, he thought to himself. On the next floor sits Mr. Quinten, Co-owner of Q.J. Enterprise. If anyone knows what to do, it would be him.

He felt the large metal box start the ascent towards his fearless leader. The clunky device moved in the most awkward manner possible. It rumbled, it shook, and it finally made it to its destination. Mr. Jefferson felt the sudden drop from underneath as the elevator connected with the third floor. He heard the ding, but the doors never opened. Instead, another blackout prevented his escape.

He edged toward the rear until his back connected with the handrail. His body slowly slid down the wall. He sat with his legs curled in his arms and began to rock back and forth. Thick tears streamed down his face, a small trickle at first, then the floodgate opened near his eye sockets. His worst fear had happened. Claustrophobia set in.

Visions of the elevator cable snapping and him falling to his demise twisted his imagination and clouded his judgment. He screamed. He pounded his fists on the metal and screamed at the top of his lungs. His throat became scratchy and raw as he repeated a single name over and over. Lindsey. No one heard his cries for help. Almost no one.

Three floors below sat a maintenance man smiling as the word Lindsey escaped from a vent in the building and echoed into the parking lot. Just when Mr. Jefferson thought he couldn't take anymore punishment, he heard the chattering once more. The chattering became louder and louder, until it was replaced with scratching noises. They were in here with him, he was sure of it.

*****

He felt something soft and fuzzy brush the side of his neck, then the side of his leg. They were everywhere! They were everywhere and nowhere all at once. Only his imagination could tell him what they looked like and how many there were. They had red glowing eyes and razor sharp teeth. They stood at least four foot of pure muscle and breathed fire. There had to be at least four thousand of them. This was for certain.

He swatted randomly at the invisible foes, thrashing here and there, but not a single squirrel fell in battle. His screams went from panic to blood-curdling in a single note. Now he was heard. Loud footsteps came charging towards the elevator on the third floor. Mr. Quinten and Mr. Johnson found their way towards the coward moments before the power came back on.

As his eyes adjusted to the light, Mr. Jefferson at last saw his rivals. Two overly cuddly squirrels lay fast asleep in the corner. He walked over towards them and kicked as hard as he could. The large black loafer came into contact with the metal, radiating pain from his foot into his hip. Cuss words came, anger rose, and his arms swung wildly. The squirrels, now agitated, attacked head on, ripping and shredding the expensive suit into many pieces. Focused on the pain and humiliation, he never noticed them disappear.

*****

Their jaws dropped. They couldn't believe what was inside the elevator. Was he overworked? Inside the elevator was a tattered, bald, Mr. Jefferson cussing and flailing wildly at nothing in particular. "Mr. Jefferson!" He turned and slowly faced his Masters. "May I ask what you are doing in there?"

He spoke through a twisted smile. "I'm bashing them good, Sir." That is all it took, he was fired on the spot. An anonymous call was made to Keeling Institute regarding Mr. Jefferson's mental state. As the two executives made it back down the hallway, oblivious of the chaos beneath, a furry brown tail flicked silently inside of Mr. Quinten's briefcase.

*****

"I know! I'm looking at the invoice sitting in front of me and I don't remember signing off on it. What do mean it has already been scheduled? This is my company and nothing goes on without my say so…Do you understand me? Who called it in? Art? Art Reddings? He is no longer with the co… Fifty dollars if I cancel? Fine! Send the Exterminator. Tomorrow afternoon. Fine, fine, I got it!"

Mr. Quinten slammed the phone down with tremendous anger, causing the receiver to bounce off of the base. After a quick adjustment, He melted deep in his chair. The Company was losing more and more money and he could feel the pinch in his back pocket. His Mahogany desk lay littered with paperwork, mostly invoices for outlandish office supplies he had to sign off on. Names. Names of the unlucky souls who made the black list of termination floated through his mind. If they cost me money, they do me no good he thought to himself.

He slowly reaches below his desk and carefully pulls the bottle of scotch from the mini-fridge, shaking his wrist to ensure his Rolex would remain scratch free. The cheery clank of the frosted glass against the desk seemed soothing. The strong burn in his stomach from the drink did little to calm his demeanor. He stared at the faux golf course overlapping his work space and decided a small break would do him some good. He pushed the paperwork to the side, almost knocking off the memo from the workers, addressed to him with the utmost concern.

His hairy wrist remained straight as he diligently swung the club. The tiny golf ball carved a perfect path towards the hole, keeping its title as the most reliable thing in his corporation. He would marvel on how it would always do exactly what he wanted and never have to be told twice. As the ball dropped into a hole in one, the satisfying click finally helped him relax enough to focus on the task at hand.

He poured himself one more drink before settling in front of the mountain of paperwork. Certain that a full day's labor was in his future, he pulled the sheet from the top of the stack and stared at it in shock. In his many years as a business man, he had never encountered anything quite like this and it frightened him.

*****

The dark sunglasses were hard to see out of. The long black wig was hot and the uniform was a little too tight. Bob stared at his reflection in the mirror with morbid fascination. My disguise as a delivery man may get me through those doors yet he thought. He readjusted the rearview in his mini-van and climbed out of driver's seat. He slowly treaded the blacktop he used to call home and headed through the gleaming doors of Q.J. Enterprises. The shrub in the lobby brought fond memories flooding back as he brought the package to the receptionist on duty. Duty…Bob snickers. He remembers the shrub in that sense as well. He recalled leaving a small brown package there too! Bob burst out laughing, bringing unneeded attention to himself. Thinking fast, he rambled an explanation to receptionist.

"I told myself a joke, as it turns out…I've never heard it before!" Bob tried to force the giggles to recede, but failed miserably. The receptionist, Brenda, as the name tag stated, didn't bother to hide the confusion she wore openly on her face.

"Can I help you Sir?"

"Um…Yes. I have a delivery for a Mr. Quinten."

"Please sign in and leave the package in receiving." She said in a monotone verse.

Sign in; sign in, Bob's mind raced as he tried to come up with a fake name. He smiled as he put the pen to the paper. The shrub still in his mind's eye, he wrote.

Gron, Ted

"Thank you, have a nice day!" Bob examined Brenda's expression for any sign of suspicion. When he was sure she was uninterested, he made his way back to the sweltering vehicle and waited, confident of his plan.

A cold piercing stare is all he could manage. The letter addressed to him had over two hundred signatures and spanned four departments. His mind raced as he tried to make sense of it all. Mr. Quinten straightened his tie and took one more swig from his magic elixir in the frosted glass. Once more he focused on the words.

Mr.Quinten,

We are unsure if you are aware of the changes that have taken place this week in your company. The work environment we endure is highly unacceptable! We have no coffee, we have no office supplies, and the rolling blackouts are making our work space increasingly hot. On top off all of that, we have no 'Enter' keys on our keyboards. Many rodents wearing what appears to be a diaper will not let us open the cabinets or icebox in the break room. We have seen two supervisors leave, a toupee dangle, and a horrible stench is coming from the fern in the lobby. We cannot take it anymore. You have until Monday to fix it or we will be on strike.

He slammed the paper down on the table and slumped in his chair. A mix between anger and sadness drained him of any energy he had left. He knew what they were talking about. The blackouts affected him as well, and he had to send his receptionist to a coffee shop every morning this week. Another day or two like this and his company may never recover. The losses were astronomical, the worst they have ever been in his company and he may not see another million dollar month.

He stood, walking through the large corridor that separated him from the lowlife workers beneath his greedy Capitalistic thumb. Since the power outages, he had to walk to his receptionist's desk anytime he needed something.

"Laurie, could you go on a coffee run for me?"

"Sure thing Mr. Quinten."

The young blonde tugged her mini-skirt down to the appropriate level before standing eye to eye with the man, knowing full well her job depended on the condition of her legs and the amount of cloth covering them. She lifted her purse from the hook and slung it over her slender shoulder. A single memo fell from the top. Laurie slowly bent over to pick up the memo, giving the pig ample time to get an eyeful. She always did this with important memos. It softened the blow of bad news and gave her…um…job security.

"Mr. Quinten, a couple of items were delivered to you this morning, they are in receiving awaiting your approval." Laurie sneered as his line of sight never left the hem of her very mini-skirt.

"Thank you Laurie, I'll head over there now."

"You're welcome Sir, oh and will you be getting the usual today?"

"Fine, Fine, that will do."

The clinking of her high heels against the marble floor brought him out of his daze. He was reminded of how great his life was up until now. Fear of losing his company, brought renewed vigor to the tasks ahead. He slowly made his way down the stairs only letting his workers see his smile. When he made it through the lobby to receiving, the overwhelming stench of the fern burned his nasal passages. They really do have it bad, don't they he thought. Well…I guess I'm glad it's not me.

Brenda gave him her biggest fake smile. "Good Morning Sir! A package was delivered by a Mr. Gron Ted. Oops…I mean Mr. Ted Gron. Also, a letter by a gentleman who claims to be Craig. I inspected his work I.D. and his real name is Conway. I'm not sure what that is about, but I took the letter for you anyway."

"Thank you Brenda."

"You're welcome sir. If there is anything thing else I can do for you just ask." Brenda once again slid a pseudo-smile his way, hoping he would notice.

"Fine fine, that will do!" Mr. Quinten took the package and the odd letter and neatly tucked it under his arm. He marched, executive style, back towards the shiny stairs.

Once out of earshot, Brenda's smile faded. "Have a heaping helping of fern, you asshole!" she mumbled through gritted teeth.

*****

The leather briefcase left tiny strips of debris among his office. After an hour of gnawing, Dribbles managed his stent of freedom. His large bushy tail flicked as his mind worked overtime. Then off into the wide world of office spaces he ventured. He ran under cubicles, and back into his previous workspace. Many cheers arose as everyone in the ten-cubicle radius caught glimpse of the mighty squirrel. To them, he was a hero, not a villain. He had slain the mighty Mr. Jefferson and they were thankful. The noise startled Dribbles, causing his pace to quicken by a leap or two. Finally, he found Mr. Quinten's storage locker. He immediately began stealing the tiny golf balls, hiding them in various hard to reach spaces. When he was all done, he headed out the back door. Sunlight and cool breeze ruffled his fur as he made his way back to the mighty Oak tree. As he climbed back up the branches and positioned himself, Conway sat down and smiled. His hand was already searching for the pack of cigarettes that dwelled deep in his pockets. Life was good!

*****

Mr. Quinten set the package down on his desk with a mighty thud and snatched the letter opener from the holder to his left. He held the sealed envelope up and touched the tip of his mini-sword to the paper. Then, everything went dark. Darkness engulfed the room and noise filled the air. Something furry brushed his hand and quickly retreated across the desk. When the light came back on...his letter opener was gone.

Well that was annoying! He thought to himself as he ripped open the envelope and spilled the contents upon his desk. He felt the thin paper between his fingers and it just seemed to radiate bad news. He flipped it over and began to read.

Mr. Quinten,

As you may know, we are having a problem with our electricity.

"No shit buddy!" he stammered

As your...

Once again darkness, horrible scratchy sounds, and the occasional brush with furry annoyance replaced his pleasant working environment. The lights came flooding back into the room and the letter was turned upside down in his hands. Harsh thoughts replaced any moral responses to the situation he may have had. He thrust his body out of his chair and charged the door, more annoyed than he has ever been. He turned the brass knob and yelled as loud as he could to Laurie.

"FIRE SOMEONE. FIRE SOMEONE LAURIE AND DON'T SEND THEM A CHRISTMAS HAM! I EXPECT

TO SEE TERMINATION PAPERS ON
MY DESK IN AN HOUR!"

"Who should I fire Sir?"

"ANYONE! I DON'T CARE. FIRE
SOMEONE UGLY!"

"Right away Sir!"

He relaxed deep in his chair and took
a deep breath. He poured himself a drink
and once again attempted to read the letter.

Mr. Quinten,

As you may know, we are having
problems with our electricity. As your
maintence man, I alone have the technical
background to fix the problem for good. I
will do so and save you thousands of dollars
by preventing the worker strike I have heard
so much about. I simply want a two dollar
raise for my services.

Thank you,

Craig (Conway) Smith

P.S. Someone stole the batteries out of your flashlight.

Mr. Quinten flung the letter across the room and swiped the remaining stack of paperwork off his desk. He stood up and grabbed the back of the chair and flung it as well. It landed hard with a deafening crash. He spotted the package, sitting on the edge of the desk, half on and half off. He lifted it above his head, and stopped himself before hurling it as well. He slowly replaced it to its home and inhaled sharply. He could feel his heart pounding and his blood pressure rising.

I need to relax he thought. A quick game of golf, and I will be just fine. Everything will be just fine. He looked at the disaster he created on his precious golf course. His ball was nowhere to be seen, swallowed by the aftermath of an impatient man. He sighs and walks out of his office and into the lobby. He smiles at Laurie and makes his way to his storage locker to get a fresh supply of golf balls. He reaches in and feels the cold metal of the vastly empty locker. He attempts once more, and achieves the same results.

"SON OF A BITCH!"

The sound resonates with a boom through the entire building. Everyone knows that voice and trembles before it. Everywhere, everybody and everything was stopped. Dozens of eyes stare blankly at him as he walks among the crowd of shocked onlookers. He passes the reception desk in the lobby where Brenda smiles once more.

"Is everythin..."

"Nuh uh!"

He holds his hand up in front of her face, cutting her off mid-sentence. He marches on through the lobby and into the accounting department. One brave soul attempts once again.

"Good Mornin…"

"Nope!"

He holds his hand up once more and keeps walking. Now back on the top floor, he trudges back into his office and grabs a single item. He stares only at the tiles as he approaches Laurie's desk. She puzzles at the sight of this, but knows better to ask.

"Give Conway a raise."

"Right away Sir!"

He says nothing else as he takes the stairs two at a time and makes his way back to the storage locker. Quiet whispers can be heard among the workers as they ponder the events that they are witnessing. Fear, confusion, and the occasional excitement passed for emotions among them.

Mr. Quinten stared calmly at the large locker analyzing it. Finally he pulled the golf club out from under his arm and beat it over and over again. Loud crippling sounds from metal on metal and words not yet defined by Webster's Dictionary was all the noise to be heard. After five grueling minutes, the golf club threw in the towel and bowed out. The head, hanging on for dear life, rested near the handle.

He walked, with a smile on his face, past Brenda.

"Good Morning Brenda."

"Good Morning sir."

She didn't bother to muster a smile this time, letting the confusion show. He hummed a happy hum while making his way back to his office. Once there, he laid the battered putter to rest among the golf course graveyard he created. Back on track, he lifted the package and tore into the brown paper surrounding it.

Seven black and white photos were neatly bunched up inside. Pictures of squirrels, big and small stared up at him. Some were stealing office supplies, and others were stealing keys off of keyboards. One in particular shocked him, a picture of a squirrel terrorizing poor Mr. Jefferson in the elevator. A letter with no signature lay beneath

I know what is happening here and I have the power to stop it. Workers are going to strike and investors will hear about it. You will lose everything. I want two million dollars. I want this by Monday or it will get worse. I will be watching!

He stood and ran. He ran to Laurie and slid the paper in front of her. He puffed and puffed for oxygen, and was finally able to speak.

"He's here! Call security!"

*****

Jonathan kept his feet high up on the chair. He never moved and hardly spoke. The guard shack was the easiest job in the company, but with mediocrity comes low pay. He didn't mind though, he spent his days checking work badges and watching television. His favorite show just started and he didn't want to miss anything, but that's how it goes. His arch nemesis, Mr. Quinten, bringer of work and all things unholy and minimum wage; just set off his radio. "Security...krrr...krrr." Jonathan stretched his arm to his waist to retrieve the radio that remained at his hip. He was worried he may have to move his legs to reach it, but was relieved when his thumb bumped the clasp.

"This is security."

"Lock down the parking lot and search the area. We have a vandal on the loose."

"Yes Sir. I will snoop around."

The theme song was just winding down when he decided to let his feet touch the concrete. He hit the switch that lowered the flimsy aluminum arm across the exit. He grabbed his flashlight and mace and slowly made his way across the parking lot. It's times like this that I hate my job he thinks. He glances back at the flimsy arm and notices it bowing in the middle. The wind makes mini waves and an ominous splooshing sound radiates from it. Yea…that will stop them. Two tons of steel will hit that and stop in an instant. The criminals will get out and hold their head between their hands and say "I would have been fine if someone didn't deploy the aluminum arm of death."

If that doesn't do the trick, certainly a security guard that weighs a hundred and twenty pounds, and reaches the enormous height of five foot six, armed with a flashlight and mace will thwart any attempts to cause mischief. Jonathan let his mind drift as he shined the light in every vehicle looking for intruders. A couple taking a long lunch break passed their work I.D.'s to him and he moved on. Everything seemed very quiet. As he passed the entrance to the office, he decided ten minutes of walking was all he could handle comfortable. He sat down on the sidewalk and looked around. Nothing out of the ordinary struck his fancy.

The birds and squirrels played a game of hide and seek. The bee's were hard at work spreading pollen here and there. Even the employees who took a late lunch settled back inside. Everything seemed perfectly…well, boring. Jonathan noticed the maintence man sitting down and staring intently at the oak tree, waiting for it to speak or talk or something.

"You there! Do you have some I.D.?"

Craig just smiled and pulled out his wallet.

"You know I do Jonathan. Who let you out of your box?"

"Ha-ha, very funny. I was sent on a very important mission to annoy you."

Craig handed him a cigarette and lit one himself.

"Making you earn your buck fifty are they?"

"They are convinced some maniac is stalking the company."

"I have found no sign of life out here, besides you that is."

Craig stared hopefully at Dribbles. If he chose this particular moment to make a cameo, than their game of cat and mouse would have to come to an end.

"Well…No time like the present. I'm off to search the back row. Hopefully, I can still catch the last ten minutes of my show."

"Wow, you really do have it bad, don't you?"

"Bite me Conway!"

Craig watched the odd little guard bounce along the parking lot shining beam after beam into cars.

*****

Bob never saw it coming. He was so fixated on what was happening inside that he forgot to pay attention. Three cars down a young man was closing in on him with his flashlight. After about five minutes, the tapping on the glass brought his attention back to the outside world. Bob slowly rolled his window down and stared at the security guard.

"Do you have your I.D. Sir?"

"I'm sure I have it here somewhere."

Bob searched his glove-box, looked under his seat, and even pulled the visor down and went through the paperwork. He was busted and he knew it.

"Well...Do you have it or don't you?"

"I'm sorry, I guess I lost it."

"Of course you did Sir."

Jonathan pulled the ugly green notepad from his pocket and produced an ink-pen. "What's your name sir?"

Thinking quick Bob came up with another fake identity. Remembering the roster of names he would send emails out for, he chose one at random.

"Jonathan Carr."

The security guard did not look amused. He simply tapped his name tag and looked at him dumbfounded.

"Nice try Sir, but there is only one Jonathan Carr here and he looks dashing in his uniform!"

"If I can't verify that you are here for work, you will be escorted to jail, so cut the crap and tell me your name!"

The loud voice caused him to drop his notepad. From behind him came the squelch of Conway.

"He's with me! He's the new maintence man. I told him to keep an eye on the second floor and let me know when the power goes out so I can flip the breaker."

Jonathan stared once more at poor Bob and then looked back at Craig.

"He's a weird one, isn't he? Make sure he has a badge by Monday, understand?"

Craig shook his head and watched Jonathan hurry off towards his guard shack. His show is nearing the end, so it would be unlikely to see him again.

Conway tapped on Bob's window, causing his panic to rise once again.

"Don't worry, I'm not here to cause you trouble."

"Thank you!" Bob sighed uneasily and softened his stiff body.

"I know it was you that has been releasing those squirrels."

"I'm afraid I don't know what you are talking about Sir!"

"Of course you don't! I just wanted to thank you. Every since you have arrived, my job has been so much more enjoyable. Now leave, before you are spotted again. They know you are here."

Craig watched the mini-van make it out of the parking lot and into the highway. His exhaust leaving evidence of foul play, but, he will never tell!

*****

Operation Extermination

The black Firebird rolled down the highway exceeding ninety miles per hour. The blue and red lights colored the day. Seven of New York's finest police-man was in hot pursuit, armed with the booming siren of justice; they closed in on the maniac. As the dotted yellow lines started to blur, they watched in horror as the sports car darted back and forth into oncoming traffic. A rather large delivery truck bumped the curb and rolled into the grass. Smoke and dirt rose high into the air and directly attacked the officer's window. Now blind, he had no choice. Officer Ace Bradley pulled the hefty shotgun from the holder behind his partners back. As he stuck his head out of the window and took aim, the constant blaring of car horns reminded him of the danger he was putting innocent bystanders in. He has only one chance to get it right, only one bullet to stop this deranged criminal. The bullet disappeared into the chamber as he pulled down on the pump action Shot gun.

Jonathan Carr thought he was watching his favorite show in surround sound; it took only a moment longer to notice the large van idling at the security gate. Always when I get to the best part! He thinks to himself. The enormous plastic bug hinged to the roof was a dead giveaway that this was indeed the exterminator, but that wasn't the point. He had to miss the ending; he had to pull his feet off of the counter and stand-up. It's Saturday for Christ sake.

"Do you have an I.D. buddy?"

"You have got to be kidding me! Do you not see the large dead bug?"

The man slaps the plastic insect, making a hollow thud ring out.

"Do I look like I have a sense of humor Sir? No I.D. No entrance." Jonathan pulls off the best monotone smirk to match the voice.

After a long irritating silence, the man passes a shiny identification card through the window. Jonathan looks it over and hands it back.

"Carries Kill Center. Are you Carrie?"

"Do I look like Carrie?"

"Looks can be deceiving sir…Where is Carrie?"

"How the hell should I know?"

"Because you work for her…or you are her, which is it?"

"I don't have time for this shit. Are you going to let me in?"

"Fine, but I am watching you!"

Jonathan smashes the large red button, making the flimsy aluminum arm start to rise. The man starts mouthing words through his window, but nothing could be heard through the glass. Out of sheer curiosity he sticks his head back out and stares at Carrie.

"What was that?"

"I said…Officer Ace Bradley misses the tire and the Firebird gets away!"

The tires squelch, propelling the large van into the parking lot at tremendous speeds.

"YOU ASSHOLE!"

A defeated sigh escaped him, as he sat back down and propped his feet up on the counter, his attention was back on the small black and white television set. Life was good...almost. The man in the magic box made an announcement that caused a shudder to radiate through his spine.

"Hi kids. It is now time for your favorite cuddly bear. Welcome to Big Bear Hour!"

"SON OF A BITCH!"

*****

Bob paced the floor of his lavish hotel room, not sure how to act. For days, he sat in the sweltering van, watching with glee as the corporate giant felt the sting of his vengeance. One department at a time, Dribbles led them to victory. His moment was near, he could feel it. He could feel it

[68]

and squeeze his fat fist around it. Then…then a rent-a-cop armed with a minimum wage attitude and a cheap walkie-talkie forced him to leave. His babies were still in there, trapped like a common rodents. He needed to get them out, today was the day! They shouldn't be in there; they will be hunted by a fat man with poison gas.

His pace picked up as the terrible thoughts drilled into his brain. Looking around the room in disgust, he longed for the nasty heat and foul smell of his van. The large television seemed to mock him from a distant, threatening an hour of enjoyment upon him. Out of curiosity, he gave in.

As the television set flipped on, he was enthusiastically greeted by the warm glow of a blue screen. Sound and picture soon followed suit. They were running a documentary on squirrel hibernation patterns, no wait…on squirrel fatalities during winter.

"Prey for Spring is brought to you by…"

Bob clicked the nasty devise off in horror, and continued to pace. He envisioned squirrels falling from the ceiling by the dozens, their diapers soiled as the nerve gas took effect. He imagined Dribbles running through the ventilation system one hop at a time, just to have an ugly head pop up and stop him in his tracks. "Where do you think you're going little fella? Mwahaha…"

Bob shook his head and willed the images away. He sat down on the edge of the king sized bed and placed his hands on his chin. I have got to get my mind straight. He thought to himself. He stared out the window for about ten minutes, taking in the view of Q.J. Enterprises across the street, before noticing the old Oak radio next to the bed. Why not? A little music would do me some good.

With a gentle click he found a station that seemed to satisfy him.

"91.3 NUTZ we're nuts for music. Up next is Alvin and the Chipmunks!"

Bob pulled the radio, plug and all, and chunked it across the room. The warm feeling of insanity started to flood his body and small chuckles tried to escape. In a panic, he throws his keys in his pocket and heads for the door. I need some air! He thinks.

*****

The van pulled into the parking spot with considerable ease. The whole place looked like a ghost town, sans the broken glass and boarded up windows. No...this ghost town had a gold encrusted mansion, infested with rodents. The man slapped the van into park and exited the vehicle. With a tug, he adjusted his coveralls and opened the back doors. With so many weapons to choose from, there was a slight delay in his actions. Finally, he lifted the magic wand attached to the pump and palmed three cans of Kill All Can Grenades. He felt around behind his toolbox until he bumped into the breathing apparatus. With a moment of struggle, the man fastened it into place, feeling like a soldier about to wade through a fog of Mustard gas.

He could hear his inhalations and smell the masks pungent odor. Through foggy plexi-glass, he watched for any sign of life. The long metal tip gleamed as it gracefully moved in a semi-circular motion in front of him. Thick fog came rolling out, coating the exterior of the doors. He watched as several crickets twitched in pain; he never understood their true purpose. He marched a soldier's march, spreading death among the insect world. One wall at a time, he started securing the perimeter. Thus blocking any attempts of escape from his foes. As he made his way around the last corner, he felt two beady eyes staring at him from the huge Oak tree.

His hand slowly reached to his belt, feeling the cold metal of a Can Grenade. His fist wrapped around it, making it ready for battle. He crept towards the tree not knowing what to expect. The light clicking of an acorn rolling down the rain gutter caused him to jump and turn his head. Another acorn followed by another echoed through the cheap aluminum pipes. Then, out of the corner of his eye, he caught sight of a brown blur hopping on the roof of the corporation. "Clever little shit, aren't you?"

With the acorns pitter-patter still ringing in his ears, he pulled the pin and chunked the grenade at the tree branch. He watched it bounce off and land nonchalantly onto the metal. He had seen it land and heard it roll, and waited for the monstrous cloud to cover the roof. Instead, all he heard was an even louder clank from the rain gutter. To his horror, the can came rolling out and stopped only a yard from him. His vision started to blur as the can continued to spew toxic fumes into the air. Through the fog and milky goggles, a bushy tail flicked and disappeared. Not missing a beat, the man shouldered his way through the doorway and took chase. Dribbles ran across the light fixtures and hopped onto support beams, but the masked man stayed only a step behind him.

*****

Spoon after spoonful went into Jonathan's mouth. Milk dribbled down his chin and the internal crunch of Cheerios rang in his ears. Loud heinous laughter erupted and his gaping mouth showed the world how skilled he was at chewing up his breakfast. His body rocked back and forth as he waited patiently to see the untimely death of the roadrunner. The fuse fizzled and the coyote was sent into a boulder at a tremendous rate of speed. Jonathan exploded with laughter once more. You would think he would start buying his products elsewhere wouldn't you? He chuckled to himself. The honking of the bird was abruptly interrupted by the honking of a Buick Sedan. Now what?

Jonathan slowly turned towards the window intent on giving that fat slob a piece of his mind. To his surprise, the part of the hideous van was being played by a quaint Buick. The smiling face of his longtime friend startled him.

"Well what do we have here? You know I can't let you in on a Saturday without authorization Craig."

"I need to get in there. It is very important that you let me in."

Jonathan rolled this over in his mind for a minute or two and came up with an astute answer

"No!"

"What do you mean no? I have to."

"Why is that? What is so important that you are willing to risk my job over?"

"Do you want me to level with you?"

"That would be the only way to gain entry…and it better be good too, I have a feeling the coyote is going to win this time. I have been waiting years for that. If I miss it, so help me…"

Craig couldn't help but like a man who centered his life around such silliness

"Do you like your job Jonathan? Would you like a raise? Better yet, how would you like it if you had to work for your money?"

"BITE YOUR TONGUE!"

"Yea, now I have your full attention."

"Do you remember the squirrels that have been causing problems?"

"Yes. The exterminator is here right now to take care of it. What about them?"

"Do you know what will happen if he kills them?"

"Everything will be back to normal. Is there a point to this?"

Craig felt like he was talking to a toddler. He bit his lip in frustration and inhaled deeply.

"Let me throw this out there for you. Things will go back to normal, except..."

"Except what? Come on Craig spit it out!"

"Mr. Quinten will have to make up the losses by cutting payroll. If he does that, Maintence and Security will be the first to be let go. We are the expendable ones. Then poor little Jonathan Carr will have to earn his keep. You will have to do more than watch television for a living!"

Jonathan could feel his chest tighten at the thought.

"What happens if the squirrels survive?"

Craig smiled and relaxed his body deep into his seat; he knew this would reel him in, hook, line, and sinker.

"Then everyone goes on strike. Mr. Quinten will need crowd control from security, and I will have to fix anything the mob breaks. This is when you can negotiate a raise."

"You are a twisted little man. But I think you are a brilliant twisted little man! Go get'em!"

Jonathan smashed the button for the second time and watched the arm slowly rise. Just as the Buick began to pull forward, Jonathan stuck his head back through the window.

"Bring me back some chips would ya?"

"You got it buddy!"

*****

"Would you like a sandwich, a salad, or a flatbread today?" Bob stared at the teen, unaware of how the store operated. So many questions, not enough answers. He bit his bottom lip and started to sweat profusely. The blonde's impatience and the ever growing crowd made concentration a mere fairy-tale. In college, Bob would study long and hard, never stopping until he had the right answer. What was the right answer? Could it be A? How about C? The answer was B, nine times out of ten it was B.

He could hear the murmurs coming from behind him, attacking him, and leaving nasty red mental bumps as they inserted their indignant stingers deep into his memory. The cashier's gaze was a heat sinking missile, Bob's pupils, the victim of a villainous plot of destruction. He could feel the heat radiating off of the florescent lights, and smell the fear pouring out of himself. How can she do this to me? The bitch! A pop quiz right in middle of public, she is the devil.

"Sir?"

"C-c-can you repeat the question?"

A puzzled look crossed the pretty face of the teen, but anxious to move things along, she immediately complied.

"Would you like a sandwich, a salad, or a flatbread today?"

"B THE ANSWER IS B! AM I RIGHT?"

"Um…sure"

Bob watched as the young lady turned and grabbed a salad bowl from the toaster behind her. As she adjusted her gloves, routine took hold.

"What kind of salad would you like?"

She immediately covered her mouth, knowing full well the damage she has just caused. To her relief, Bob started spouting off the list of ingredients he would like.

"I would like Lettuce, Walnuts, Pecans, Almonds, Cashews, and Ranch dressing please."

"Sorry sir, we don't carry those."

Devastation sprinkled with confusion sank in. Until now, his thoughts were on poor Dribbles and the squad of minions fighting a losing battle. Unaware of what he said, he tried to remain calm. Deep inside the pit of his stomach he could feel madness rising.

"I'm sorry, what don't you have Ma'am?"

"Nuts."

"I AM NOT!" at her blank stare, he realized she was not questioning his sanity, but that they didn't serve nuts. "THERE ARE DOZENS OF SQUIRRELS UNDER MY CONTROL RUNNING AMUCK. DO

THEY HAVE THE OPPORTUNITY TO EAT A SALAD? DID YOU ASK THEM IF THEY WANTED A FLATBREAD? NO. RIGHT NOW THEY NEED A DIAPER CHANGE AND FED BEFORE THEY CAN CONTINUE TO TEAR DOWN CORPORATE AMERICA AND YOU ARE GOING TO INFORM ME THAT THEIR MISSION WILL FAIL BECAUSE YOU DO NOT HAVE THE INGREDIENTS NEEDED TO MAKE A SIMPLE SALAD. "

His chest caved in and expanded as he inhaled deeply. He saw a look of terror on the poor girls face and watched her back slowly towards the door. Once she disappeared, a simple thought occurred to him. I'm losing it! I need to get them out of there right now before I cause any more trouble. He heard a small click and a deep voice came over the intercom system.

"Security Check"

"Shit!"

*****

Dribbles could feel the man's stare and hear the steady Clack of his shoes beating around behind him. His balance was impeccable as he jumped from pipe to pipe to avoid the man's rage. The florescent lights swayed to and fro as he stopped dead center to breathe. The man tried to concentrate on his furry nemesis, but could not get his eyes to focus properly. In place of the squirrel, danced red dots before his pupils. The nozzle of his sprayer aimed high as the stainless steel gleamed mockingly. Certain death came to all who were unlucky enough to catch a glimpse of that wand. Like a deer in a trance, caught in the high beams on a desolate highway, Dribbles could not break away from his stare-down. The fat finger of the city's most efficient killer slowly started to squeeze the trigger. Before the toxic cloud could spew out, the lights went out.

The spell now broken, Dribbles took off down the lights and across the pipes. The man had to go by sound alone, but could pinpoint the general location of the foul beast. One foot in front of the other, he followed the hollow echo of metal on metal as the lights collided into each other. His sprayer led the way, spilling toxins towards any unidentified sound. A thick fog started filling the dark room; another ten minutes and anything that breathes would suffer a cruel fate. He knew he had him, only one way in and one way out. The man laughs as the filter on his mask prevents poison from entering his lungs. His body slowly backs to the only exit in the room, blocking it completely. It was now simply a waiting game and he was still on the clock. After only a few minutes, he could hear the scratching on the marble floor as his arch-nemesis attempted to make a run for it. The man pulled the pin and chunked the Can-Grenade towards the ominous sound, hoping to hear the nasty thud of metal on meat.

The can rolled, screeching along the marble. An audible hiss echoed as its contents spilled out of the nozzle. A direct miss! The man's eyes strained to focus in the vast darkness. The scratching became louder, to almost deafening proportions. A tiny blur of brown fur became visible as he came face to face with his enemy for the first time. Only one of them was getting out of this room. A strange sensation came over the man, one he never expected. Large ugly dots covered his eye-sight; searing pain seemed to grow from directly underneath his cranium. His body became weak, then completely surrendered. The boom of the fat body collapsing was heard all the way at the guard shack.

*****

The hotel blinds were split apart once more as Bob's eye peered across the street at Q.J. Enterprises. To his surprise, another vehicle was parked in the lavish parking lot. He watched Conway the maintence man come walking out of the side entrance, carrying a large Crescent Wrench. Horror swelled deep inside, as violent thoughts plagued him. Bob could picture the brute swinging with all his might at his furry buddies, making contact with a horrible thud. Squirrels would fly through the air, only to land unconscious across the room. What kind of monster would do such a thing?

[84]

Bobs pace quickened. For over ten minutes now, he has been walking back and forth in front of the window uncertain of what to do. A thought occurred to him, who's side is he on? Memories of his close call had him doubting himself. Is he a friend or is he a monster?

He closed his eyes and replayed it over again in his mind.

"If I can't verify that you are here for work, you will be escorted to jail, so cut the crap and tell me your name!"

"He's with me! He's the new maintenance man. I told him to keep an eye on the second floor and let me know when the power goes out so I can flip the breaker."

"Make sure he has a badge by Monday, understand?"

Conway tapped on Bob's window, causing his panic to rise once again. "Don't worry, I'm not here to cause you trouble."

"Thank you!" Bob sighed uneasily and softened his stiff body.

[85]

"I know it was you that has been releasing those squirrels."

"I'm afraid I don't know what you are talking about Sir!"

"Of course you don't! I just wanted to thank you. Every since you have arrived, my job has been so much more enjoyable. Now leave, before you are spotted again. They know you are here."

Bob shook away the memory now certain of one thing…they needed his help. He snatched his sunglasses and threw his wallet in his pocket. Excitement and energy seemed to fill him to the core; he may get them out yet!

*****

Craig watched as the man blocked the only exit out of Q.J. Enterprises. He heard the Can-Grenade hit and slide across the marble floor. Time was limited. He inhaled deeply, taking the last drag off of his cigarette before littering the parking lot with the used butt. The orange glow of the tip sparked and expanded into many bits as it collided with the pavement.

He knew what he had to do, but it went against everything he believed in. On one hand, it is very inhumane to land a forceful blow to the back of someone's head. On the other, he has grown to love those little guys, especially the tree hugger that has made his job so simple these last few days. If the exterminator kills him then life will return to normal. I will have to use these blasted tools and pretend like I know what the hell I'm doing! Deep in thought, Craig's hand slides to the Crescent Wrench on his tool belt. He feels the cold metal in his hand as he hoists it out of its home.

"What the hell is this Chompy-Thingy McBob anyways? I may not know how to use it, but I sure know how to swing it!" He mumbles under his breath as he rears back for the attack. With all of his might, he swings at the back of the man's head. The cold steel connects with flesh and nothing happens. For a good minute solid, Craig watched the man stand his ground. Fear creeps up on him like a shadow in the night.

Any minute he will turn around and attack me. He will say something like…

"Did you think that silly little Chompy-Thingy McBob could stop me? Hahaha I am immune to Chompy-Thingy McBobs and now you will pay!"

His hand reaches back to his tool belt, feeling for anything that would make a good back up weapon. The largest item left is a simple flathead screwdriver. Without hesitation, he draws the mammoth weapon out of its makeshift sheath and wields it like a true knight. The light reflects off of a solid twelve inches of chrome, building confidence at the task ahead. His knuckles turn white as the strength of his grip increases.

"SCREW YOU!"

He closed his eyes and held his breathe waiting for the battle to begin. A loud thump took the place of the death blow he was waiting for. When he opened his eyes, the man lay upon the marble, victim of Craig the Dragon-Slayer. An audible oomph came cascading out of the brave man, as he tried to regain the normalcy of his heartbeat. He watched with delight as Dribbles led the squirrel army out of the gas chamber and into the warmth of the day. A small victory for the worker bees, but a victory none the less!

*****

Bob darted across the busy freeway, ignoring the honks and cursing radiating from oncoming traffic. With so much at stake, nothing would stop him. As he passed the arch way and made his way towards the guard shack, his body began to tremble. Too many years sitting behind a desk had made him weak, a blob of a man who, up until now avoided physical exertion at all costs. But this was important Damn it! He trudged on, forcing his body to bow to his will. He finally made it to the shack when a voice reminded him where he was.

"Whoa there buddy. It's Saturday. I can't let you in there"

Bob stared at the scrawny man wishing his head would explode.

"Humph. Humph. I gotta…humph"

"You gotta lay off of the cheeseburgers, that's what you got to do. I told you already, no one is allowed in there today."

"It's an emergency. I have to get in or else…"

"Or else what? Or else your squirrels will die?"

Bob stood in shocked silence. For the first time all day, his brain didn't want to respond to the situation at hand.

"Listen, pal personally I'm with you. Down with the man and all of that jazz, but I can't risk letting you in. If you get caught then it's my ass and I intend on getting paid to watch the road-runner meet his demise."

"How can I save them then? What about Dribbles, What about the exterminator? What about…"

"It's all taken care of. Come Monday morning, Mr. Quinten will have a strike on his hands."

"How do you know this? Right now there could be…"

"Shh…just trust me, everything will work out."

It was at that particular moment that Bob heard the loud thump and watched his minions escape with their lives. Everything did work out. This guard is a genius!

"I will see you Monday then?"

*****

Operation Monday

The Black Limo pulled onto the lot at 6:57 am. A full two hours prior to the normal time he would stroll into the office. His cell phone rang and his lowly workers informed him that there was "a situation". Mr. Quinten chuckled to himself. Of course there is! There has been! The situation is that I'm now staring through the tinted glass of a limo as half my staff are calling me names that even I never heard.

A small humming came from the window as it slowly slid down, exposing his beady eyes. His glance was fierce and unyielding as he tried to pinpoint the leader of the office rebels. Daring to expose himself further, he let the window disappear completely.

The fresh air licked at his face and the sounds of chanting verbally assaulted his ears. Dozens of men and women marched back and forth in their office attire, hoisting signs that ranged from " Fair work conditions for all" to "The devil has private cubicles".

After some time he spotted a friendly face, one loyal worker bee who could help him get to the bottom of this. He smiled as he seen Laurie's pretty face. Dressed nicely and ready for work. Punctual. that was one of the things he admired about her. Always loyal and on time ready to serve the better good of Q.J. Enterprises.

He stuck his head slowly out of the extraordinarily overpriced company car and raised his voice over the chants. Calling her.

"Laurie!! Hey come here I need you." he shouted

He watched her smile and stroll closer to the Limo. Relief washed over him like hot water washing away dirty stains on muddy blue jeans.

As she stepped closer to him her smile disappeared from her pretty face and her mouth twisted into an angry smirk.

"HERE IS YOUR COFFEE SIR!" she yelled as she slung the hot liquid, cup and all at the limo. He felt the impact and heard the glass shatter, searing pain climbed up his nerve endings. His clothes covered with dark brown liquid, he could hear the cheers rise from the crowd. Closing the window he looked up at the driver.

"Take me home, I have a few calls to make." he flatly stated.

"I can't Sir"

"Why not?"

The driver pocked the keys and opened up the driver side door, leaving the man stranded in a sea of angry worker bees, letting the stinger of vengeance inch ever closer.

"Cause I'm on strike Sir!"

*****

Craig smirked through his well groomed handlebar mustache. He watched as the glass shattered against the side of the limo. Food wrappers, Styrofoam cups, and cigarette butts littered the pavement. He leaned against the side of the building and pulled the radio from his pocket. Pressing the button firmly he spoke.

"Looks like the maintence department is getting overtime"

a static voice crawled over the airwaves.

"I still haven't received a call there good buddy." Jonathan stated.

"Give it time, the crowd is getting restless."

"I will give it twenty three minutes, give or take a commercial break."

Jonathan leaned back in his chair and turned the channel, ready to see the coyote finally catch that stupid ass bird. He jumped as he heard the guard shacks phone ring in the background. Sitting up, he slowly lifted the receiver to his ear, knowing all too well who was going to be on the other end.

"Security, This is Jonathan" He spoke through a grin

Panic seeped through the commanding voice.

"This is Mr. Quinten, I need you for crowd control."

"No can do Mr. Quinten."

"Wait...what? You are security Jonathan. Come do crowd control or your fired!"

"I'll think about it Mr. Quinten, but there is two hundred of them and only one of me. Besides...How do you know I'm not on strike myself?"

He could hear the anger creep up in Mr. Quintens voice.

"You listen here you little shit. If you are not down on the lot in ten minutes YOU ARE FIRED! DO YOU HEAR ME? FIRED."

"Uh huh, Fired got it. I will think about it." Jonathan slowly hung up the receiver and leaned back in his chair. He watched the cartoon fade and commercial break interrupt him. A new found hatred for Mr. Quinten swelled.

"I missed it!" he said to no one in particular.

Lifting the radio to his lips he spoke to his wrench-totting fool of a buddy.

"I hope you know what you are doing. If you're wrong I'm fired!"

"Be patient. Things are in motion as we speak."

*****

The crowd engulfed the limo like a ants to a morsel. Mr. Quinten could feel his body jar as the massive vehicle rocked back and forth. His impenetrable armor of corporate courage split leaving his vulnerable heart wide open. He could feel fear. He could feel regret. Was this what it was like to have a conscience? The thought turned his mind to mush.

He could feel himself flinch at the onslaught of vulgar insults and taunts. This was insanity! Where is security? Mr. Quinten tried to look beyond the crowd but alas, the mass of worker bees were too much. He fumbled for his phone, his chest still struggling for oxygen he could feel his warm breath escape in clumps.

"Security this is Jonathan" He spoke unconcerned.

"Well hello again Mr. Quinten. What can I do for you?"

The limo started to lift every so slightly from the ground. Vertigo and crippling fear steered the conversation. Mr. Quinten was losing emotional control.

"Where are you? I need crowd control now! They are trying to tip the car over on me." He whispered.

Jonathan smiled and leaned back, reeling in his invisible fishing pole; he had the man hook line and sinker.

"I'm at the guard shack Mr. Quinten. Hold on just a second okay?"

"WAIT! DON'T PUT ME ON..."

Jonathan placed the receiver down and grabbed the binoculars from the large wooden desk. He chuckled as he spotted the limo being rocked, wheels void of pavement and a large blobby mass of a person pin balling back and forth on unscuffed leather seating. A perfect sight!

He put the binoculars down and lifted the receiver slowly to his ear.

"Mr. Quinten?"

"Don't you ever put me on hold again you little..." his sentence was cut off sharply by Jonathans monotone response.

"You are right as usual boss." He spoke

"What are you talking about? I don't have time for these games."

"It does in fact appear your limo is being tipped Mr. Quinten. Did you really need me to verify that for you? Be honest boss, you could have figured that much out on your own."

"I KNOW I'M BEING TIPPED YOU MORON. I NEED YOUR HELP."

"Can't" Jonathan flatly stated

"Why not? It's your job!" Mr. Quinten felt himself fluster and his voice stutter ever so slightly.

"I thought I was fired Mr. Quinten?"

"No your not fired. Matter of fact, we need men like you. Men with integrity! Now please come and control the crowd."

"Can't"

Jonathan smiled and kicked up his feet. He clicked the tiny knob on his cheap television and smacked the side, trying to will it to work better.

Mr. Quinten felt the limo raise even higher. In only a matter of minutes, the company car and his own personal safety will be in question. He could see the look on Laurie's face. Unconcerned. Happy. She was almost ecstatic to see him in his current situation. That bitch! he thought.

"Your not fired! I-I'm thinking of giving you a raise actually."

"I'm listening...how much boss man?"

" Twenty five cents. Will give you a quarter raise and promote you to head of security!"

Jonathan gasped for breath and tears streamed down his eyes at the sentiment. Was he really this dumb? The great and powerful Mr. Quentin, unaware that I am the ONLY security guard. Head of security Bah. I will manage to manage myself? Maybe I'll fuck up and fire myself? Or I will make myself do the shit work so I don't have to do it. Jonathan continued to laugh.

"I wasn't joking a raise."

He could feel the limo threaten to tip, only a few more minutes and he was toast. Time was running out and his negation tactics were failing him.

"What do you say? Want a raise? Come help me out and the position is all yours."

Jonathan thought very carefully...

"Nah I think I'm on strike."

Jonathan hung up the receiver and slowly poured himself a cup of stale coffee. Kicking his feet up he was not surprised to hear the phone ring once more.

"Former security. Leave message at the beep!"

"WAIT! DON'T HANG UP. A LARGER RAISE ! ANYTHING YOU WANT, JUST GET ME OUT OF HERE"

Mr. Quinten felt himself sob. Anger, Frustration, fear, and regret bombarded him all at once.

"Anything I want Mr. Quinten?"

Jonathan felt like jumping for joy. This was going to be fun. The crazy maintence man was right.

"ANYTHING. YES YES NOW GET ME OUT OF HERE!"

"you promise?"

"OF COURSE NOW HELP ME"

"say I promise you anything you want"

"ARE YOU SHITTING ME? YES I PROMISE YOU ANYTHING YOU WANT NOW HELP."

"On my way boss man."

Jonathan grabbed the bullhorn and hopped on the golf cart, trying everything he could to burn rubber.

" I will get a new golf cart while I'm at it. One with big knobby tires and a lift kit. yes!"

*****

The sound of his heavy metal tools pinging off of the sidewalk etched itself into his memory. He will never again be the maintence man. Never again will he go by any other name than his own. He could see the white dot crawl closer and closer as Jonathan's cart pulled onto the lot.

Craig sat against the rough bricks and lit a smoke, inhaling deeply, he felt freedom mix with the nicotine. Pulling out his radio for the very last time he rubbed it slowly against his handlebar mustache and spoke.

"Well done."

****

The crowd didn't register the words coming from the bullhorn at first. They seemed so out of place among the greed, discrimination, and torture they all have come to expect at Q.J. Enterprises. After the third attempt, The crowd simmered do to a quiet boil and concentrated on the news they were given.

"Attention   Q.J.   Enterprise employees. Mr. Quinten has decided it was time for a change in the hierarchy of management and has graciously appointed me C.E.O. of Q.J. Enterprises. I thank you all for your hard work and want to start things off right. As of this moment all of you will be given a paid week of vacation and a raise. Go home. Come back next Monday and things will be back to normal. Thank you and enjoy."

Jonathan smiled as the crowd scattered away from the limo and the protests of injustice was replaced by the hushed rustling of the oak trees. The light clicking of Laurie's high heels reminded him of one final misdeed that needed fixed.

"Laurie! Laurie hold up a second!" He stated through the bullhorn.

The lady turned and smiled at him, Not quite sure how to handle the events that just unfolded before her eyes.

"Yes sir?"

"Don't call me Sir please." he spoke

"Sorry Sir."

Jonathan just shook his head and finished his thought

"When you applied here you originally applied for a much greater position but was denied because you have..certain attributes that Mr. Quinten found to be desirable in a secretary. Am I right?"

She blinked. Almost astonished at the bluntness of this conversation.

"Yes Sir. I suppose so" she stared at the concrete.

"I want you to do one final task for me as a secretary, you do that and come Monday morning I will give you the position you applied for. Interested?"

He watched Laurie's eyes shine with hope.

"Yes Sir! What will you have me do?"

"Do you remember Bob from accounting?"

"Vaguely Sir." she flustered

"Pull his file, and write him a conditional offer of employment, starting him as Full Partner in the firm."

"Right away Sir."

He watched her bounce along the sidewalk with both purpose and haste. Joy. Excitement. Freedom. As she disappeared into the distance, entering through the golden doors as secretary for the very last time, Jonathan tapped on the glass of the limo.

Mr. Quinten slowly lowered it, ready to have war with the scrawny security guard. Instead, He felt the weight of the bullhorn slam in his lap, along with a voice recorder.

"I have copies. You promised me anything. Disagree and I will see you in court."

Jonathan walked away ignoring the obscenities streaming from overpriced vehicle. Starting the golf cart, his final thoughts as a lowly security guard facing the very last Monday in his career was simplistic.

I wonder if I missed the coyote catching the road-runner?